Elfa and the Box of Memories

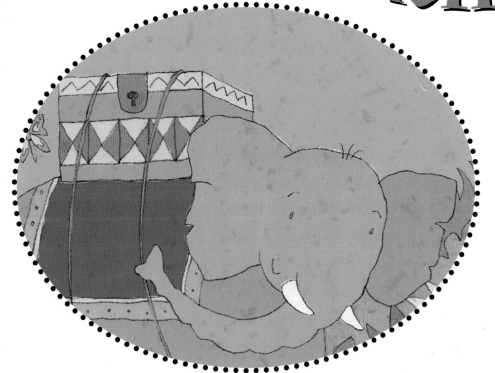

Michelle Bell

Illustrations by Rachel Fuller

823.92

Published by
British Association for Adoption & Fostering (BAAF)
Saffron House
6–10 Kirby Street
London EC1N 8TS
www.baaf.org.uk

Charity registration 275689 (England and Wales)
and SCO39337 (Scotland)

British Library Cataloguing in Publication Data
A catalogue record for this book is available from
the British Library

ISBN 978 1 905664 42 9

Project management by Shaila Shah, BAAF
Illustrations by Rachel Fuller
Designed and typeset by Andrew Haig & Associates
Printed in Great Britain by the Lavenham Press
Trade distribution by Turnaround Publisher Services,
Unit 3, Olympia Trading Estate, Coburg Road,
London N22 6TZ

Printed on FSC certified, chlorine-free paper

The author
Michelle Bell works part-time as BAAF's
Publications Marketing Officer. She lives in
south-east London with her husband and three
young children. *Elfa and the box of memories*
is her first children's book.

The illustrator
Rachel Fuller specialises in children's books and
developing and illustrating novelty packages as well
as young fiction and educational materials.

For Gemma, Ruby and Daisy –
making special memories every day

Michelle Bell

For my good friends Sandra and Paul
and their three children Lana, Kyra and Anya

Rachel Fuller

Elfa the Elephant was in a bad mood. It was a hot day and she was carrying a box on her back. It was really heavy and felt very uncomfortable. It had just got stuck in the low branches of a tree and Elfa's ears got scratched as she struggled to set it free.

3

Elfa carried the box on her back everywhere she went. She never took it off because she was scared of losing it. But even though it was a beautiful shiny box, none of the other animals ever seemed to notice or ask what was inside it.

They didn't know that inside the box Elfa kept her most precious things — her memories. It was full of special reminders of the places where she had lived, the animals that had looked after her and important things that had happened.

A group of warthogs came running out of
the trees and asked Elfa if she wanted to play. Elfa
happily joined in. She ran around as fast as she could and
jumped out of the way as the ball came whizzing past.
Suddenly one of the bigger warthogs kicked the ball hard
towards Elfa. It hit the box on her back and made the
sharp edges dig into her skin.
'Owww!' cried Elfa.
'That really hurt.'

The big warthog sniggered and didn't say sorry. It was all too much for Elfa – she started to shout and stamp her feet. The warthogs looked at each other in surprise. They didn't know what to do. The ball had only hit the box on Elfa's back. Why was she so angry?

Just then Marvin the wise monkey swung down from the top of a
tall tree. 'What's up, Elfa?' he asked and offered her a banana.
And that's when it all came tumbling out – Elfa couldn't
stop herself. She told Marvin about how cross she was that
nobody ever asked her about her box. That it was full of
her most precious memories and that sometimes she just
wanted to talk about them with someone else.

'Oh Elfa,' sighed Marvin, 'I'd love to share your memories with you. Let's go and find a shady spot, open up your box and you can tell me all about the special things you keep inside.' Elfa was pleased that Marvin wanted to share her memories.

They found a comfortable place to sit, and Elfa used her trunk to lift down the heavy box. She carefully opened the lid. There were so many memories crammed inside — happy memories that made Elfa smile, sad memories that made her cry, funny memories that made her laugh and angry memories that made Elfa cross and want to flap her ears.

Suddenly Elfa noticed that there were some strange gaps in the great big jumble of memories. Oddly shaped holes where she knew memories used to be - she just couldn't remember what they were. It had been so long since Elfa had looked at her memories. Some of them had simply faded away.

Elfa's eyes filled with tears. 'Some of my memories are missing. I've lost them. What am I going to do?' she cried.

'No problem,' replied Marvin with a great big grin. 'I'll help you find those missing memories and fill your box again. We just need to look in the right places!'

The next morning Elfa and Marvin set off to visit the nursery where she had lived just after she was born. All the nurses remembered Elfa. They told her how she loved to be cuddled and always giggled when they sang "Nelly the Elephant".

One of the nurses gave Elfa a copy of her footprint, which they had made when she was just a few weeks old. It was bright purple and in a few places the paint had dribbled and splodged, but Elfa loved it and she carefully put it in to her box.

15

Then they took a trip to the doctor's. Elfa wasn't feeling poorly – she was going to see if the doctor could help her with her missing memories.

Dr Noceros looked in a big blue folder with Elfa's name on the front. It was full of pieces of paper covered in scribbly writing. 'Aha,' he said. 'This looks like something for you.' He handed Elfa a large sticker. On it was a spotty face and the words "You've been brave".

'Do you remember when you had the elly-spots?' asked Dr Noceros. 'You were covered in them, from the tops of your ears to the tip of your tail. They were so itchy, but you did what you were told and never scratched them.' The thought of the elly-spots made Elfa's skin feel very prickly. She proudly stuck the sticker inside her box.

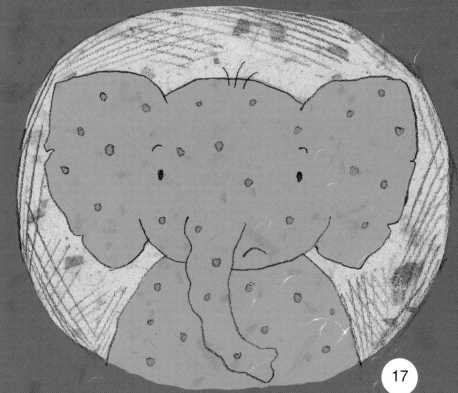

A few days later, Elfa and Marvin went to see Harry and Helen Hippo. Elfa had lived with them for many happy months and they were really pleased to see her again. As they tucked in to a feast of cream cakes, juicy fruit and wobbly jellies – all Elfa's favourites – they chatted about the time that they had spent together.

When it was time to leave, Harry and
Helen hugged Elfa and gave her a photo taken
at her first birthday party.

The photo made Elfa feel sad. There was a tickle in her trunk and
she wanted to cry. She had been so happy with Harry and Helen
and she hadn't wanted to leave them. She still didn't understand
why they couldn't look after her forever. Marvin lifted the lid of
the box and Elfa gently put the photo inside.

Finally they visited Greenleaf Primary School. Elfa recognised her old teacher, Miss Hightree, but she couldn't remember anything else about the school. Standing in the playground, Miss Hightree showed Elfa a shiny gold medal on a red ribbon and a certificate that said "1st Place".

'You won these when you were the captain of our Tail Tug-of-War team. Everyone was so proud when Greenleaf came first in the schools competition.' Elfa couldn't believe she had forgotten being captain of the winning team. She slipped the medal around her neck and put the certificate inside her box.

Now all the gaps in Elfa's box of memories were full again. 'Thank you Marvin,' she said. 'I would never have been able to remember all those special times on my own. It's not easy when you haven't got anyone to share your memories with.'

'Well now you've got me,' smiled Marvin. 'I really enjoyed finding out about the things that happened to you when you were growing up. Any time you want to share some of your memories, just look for me up in the treetops. I'll swing down straight away.'

Elfa was very proud of her box, especially now that it was bursting with memories again. Marvin helped her find somewhere safe to keep it – a secret hiding place in the shady spot where she had first shared her memories with him.

Now she could play with the other animals and run through the trees without worrying about the heavy box on her back.

And she knew that she could never forget her memories because she could share them with her wise friend Marvin.